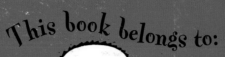
This book belongs to:

JANE vs. the Tooth Fairy

by **Betsy Jay**
illustrated by **Lori Osiecki**

rising moon

The black line work for the illustrations were done by traditional scratchboard technique,
then the illustrations were scanned and digitally painted in Photoshop.
The text and display type were set in Fontesque
Composed in the United States of America
Designed by Michael Russell
Edited by Aimee Jackson
Production supervised by Lisa Brownfield
Printed in Hong Kong by Wing King Tong Company Limited

www.northlandpub.com

FIRST IMPRESSION
ISBN 0-87358-769-3

Library of Congress Cataloging-in-Publication Data
Jay, Betsy, 1978-Jane vs. the tooth fairy / by Betsy Jay ; illustrated by Lori Osiecki.
        p.   cm.
    Summary: Jane's mom and grandmother tell her that the Tooth Fairy will pay her
money for her loose wiggly tooth, but Jane decides that she would rather keep the tooth.
    ISBN 0-87358-739-1
    [1.Tooth Fairy—Fiction. 2. Teeth—Fiction.] I. Title: Jane versus the tooth fairy.
II. Osiecki, Lori, ill. III. Title.

PZ7.J3295 Jan 2000
[E]—dc21   00-021028

79/7.5M/6-00

For John, Dean, and Marietta.

—B. J.

To my short people, Alex and Max.

—L. O.

One night my tooth started wiggling in my mouth. I was brushing my teeth with my pink-sparkle  bubblegum toothpaste when it happened. I ran to tell Momma right away so we could get me to the doctor. I thought there was something very wrong with me and maybe I needed a cast or stitches. She wasn't worried. She said, "Oh, Jane, you're losing your first tooth! You're such a big girl these days." Then she and Daddy wanted to look at it in my mouth. They were both very excited. Neither one of them has a loose tooth. All their teeth stand still.

I was standing in the yard while Momma talked to Mr. Henley across the fence. Momma said, "Come show Mr. Henley your loose tooth." So I walked over there and opened my mouth for him. That was when he wiggled it and said, "I've got just the thing for that." He picked up a yard tool that pulled things and acted like he would pull out my tooth with it. I thought he might be teasing, but I screamed and ran away from him anyway, just to be safe. I don't want anybody to take out my tooth, no matter how wiggly it gets or if I can't even chew with it. I've had this tooth forever and I'm keeping it.

Grandma came the next day to visit for a week, and I still had the loose tooth. She sleeps in the other bed in my room. My grandma is an old woman, but she has lots of tricks. She can take her teeth out and her hair off. When she sleeps, she keeps her hair on a fake head and puts her teeth in a little glass. I've been watching her carefully in case she takes something else off, like a leg or a head.

I went to the toy store with Momma and Grandma. Grandma gave me ten dollars and said, "You buy whatever you want with this money." What I wanted was an art set with crayons, markers, and paints. Momma said I'd need another $3.50 to buy the art set. Then I remembered my loose tooth and I told her I wanted to buy some dentures like Grandma's, only smaller. Momma said they don't make dentures for little girls. Little girls have to grow their teeth back when they lose them. I don't think that's fair. I told Momma I've decided to go ahead and keep this tooth, even if it does wiggle.

A mean boy at my school, Jimmy, has a loose tooth, but he likes his. He told me the tooth fairy will come and take it away while he is sleeping and leave him money. After he told me that I knew it must be the tooth fairy who makes my tooth loose. I thought she must come in my room at night and pull on it until it wiggles.

Now I sleep with the window closed and my mouth shut so the tooth fairy can't get in. I thought it was an awfully good thing that Grandma's teeth were in that glass right on the table in case the tooth fairy got in after all. If I were the tooth fairy, I would take Grandma's teeth first because they are so much fancier than mine are. I told Grandma about this, and she said the tooth fairy wouldn't do that. She said the tooth fairy only takes away teeth someone else doesn't need any more. I don't believe her.

I don't think pulling out teeth is a very nice thing for the tooth fairy to do, even if she does leave me money for it, and even if she wears a fairy costume with diamonds on it and has a magic wand. It's my tooth, and if she pulls it out I'm going to have to go to all the trouble of growing it back. Everybody acts like the tooth fairy is some friendly person. I don't think she is. If I went around pulling out people's teeth, I would probably have to go to jail. I know this because I tried pulling out Jimmy's tooth during naptime, and I had to sit in the corner all through recess.

Momma had to go to the dentist, and she made me go with her. Inside the dentist's office there is a big stool shaped like a tooth, but much bigger, that you can sit on. I sat on it. There is a picture of the tooth fairy on the wall. I said, "This dentist must like the tooth fairy." The lady behind the desk said, "Oh, yes. The dentist and the tooth fairy are close personal friends." Then I made my mouth shut as tight as I could and gave Momma a look to let her know that I would not be opening my mouth the rest of the time we were there. She thought I was being silly, but I was being safe with my teeth.

Grandma told me that all her teeth fell out because she didn't brush them enough, so I figured out that since brushing teeth keeps them from falling out, I could brush my tooth back into standing still. All day long I brushed my teeth every time I remembered to. I used a whole tube of pink-sparkle bubblegum toothpaste. When I brushed the tooth it kept getting looser and looser, so I had to keep brushing it harder and harder to try to make it stay in, until I brushed it so hard it brushed right out of my mouth and into the sink. It didn't hurt much, but it had blood on it, so I screamed.

Everybody came running, and when they saw that my tooth was out, they were happy and they told me I was a big girl. It felt funny in my mouth where my tooth used to be. I kept the tooth in my pocket all day with a wishbone from a turkey and an army man with a purple outfit that I painted on him all by myself.

I played with the tooth all day, but I found out there isn't much you can do with a tooth once it's outside your mouth. I wished I had the art set from the toy store. That's when I got my idea. Momma said the tooth fairy pays a dollar for a tooth. My tooth would have to get fancy to pay for the rest of the art set. I found a blue marker and colored it all over, and Grandma helped me glue some sequins on it from my old dance costume.

When it was time for bed, I put it under my pillow.

I put a note under there, too. It said:

Dear Tooth Fairy,
    This is a very fancy
tooth for you. It costs
$3.50. Take it
or leave it.
    Sincerely,
    Jane

P.S. If you don't
buy it my
Grandma
will.

The next morning the tooth was gone and I found $3.50 under my pillow instead. I ran to show Momma and Daddy. They said, "The tooth fairy must think your teeth are very fancy." I told them, "The tooth fairy and I are close personal friends."

Betsy Jay grew up in Waynesville, North Carolina, with her brother and two sisters. She now attends the University of North Carolina at Wilmington, majoring in Education.

Betsy remembers losing about twenty-six teeth over the course of her childhood. Though Betsy did cash in most of her baby teeth, after awhile she began saving them to keep in her pockets and to make necklaces with. When she started working on *Jane vs. the Tooth Fairy*, Betsy knew that Jane would be much more assertive about marking this rite of passage in a way that emphasized her creativity and independence.

Betsy now lives in Wilmington, North Carolina, with her husband.

Lori Osiecki was born in Shillington, Pennsylvania, and attended the York Academy of Arts. She worked for Hallmark Cards, Inc., for eight years before moving to Arizona and becoming a freelance illustrator. Lori has illustrated numerous books, including *Swimming Lessons*, Rising Moon's first "Jane" book in the series.

While this book was being made, Lori's daughter, Alex (seven), lost her two front teeth. Unlike Jane, Alex decided that keeping her teeth was better than trading them for the money. She already had a paint set.

Lori lives in Mesa, Arizona, with her son Max, her daughter Alex, and their dog, George (who refused to get into the spaceship for the picture).